Lulu Bell and the Tiger Cub

A Random House book
Published by Random House Australia Pty Ltd
Level 3, 100 Pacific Highway, North Sydney NSW 2060
www.randomhouse.com.au

First published by Random House Australia in 2014

Addresses for companies within the Random House Group can be found at
www.randomhouse.com.au/offices

National Library of Australia
Cataloguing-in-Publication Entry

Author: Murrell, Belinda
Title: Lulu Bell and the tiger cub/Belinda Murrell; illustrated by Serena Geddes
ISBN: 978 0 85798 301 5 (paperback)
Series: Murrell, Belinda. Lulu Bell; 7
Target audience: For primary school age
Subjects: Zoos – Juvenile fiction
Tiger cubs – Juvenile fiction
Monkeys – Juvenile fiction
Other authors/contributors: Geddes, Serena
Dewey number: A823.4

Cover and internal illustrations by Serena Geddes
Cover design by Christabella Designs
Internal design and typesetting in 16/22 pt Bembo by Anna Warren, Warren Ventures
Printed in Australia by Griffin Press, an accredited ISO AS/NZS 14001:2004 Environmental Management System printer

Random House Australia uses papers that are natural, renewable and recyclable products and made from wood grown in sustainable forests. The logging and manufacturing processes are expected to conform to the environmental regulations of the country of origin.

Lulu Bell and the Tiger Cub

Belinda Murrell

Illustrated by Serena Geddes

RANDOM HOUSE AUSTRALIA

Molly
Lulu
Dad

Mum
Gus
Rosie

To all the wonderful teachers who have inspired my kids over the years – thank you!

Chapter 1

Zoo Excursion

Lulu hopped from foot to foot to keep warm. Her backpack bumped up and down on her back. Overhead the sky was heavy with dark grey clouds.

It was Wednesday morning and everyone was at school super-early. Lulu felt a bubble of excitement in her tummy. Today was the day of the big zoo adventure.

All the year three students from Shelly Beach School were going on the excursion. It was extra special for Lulu because the zoo vet, Dr Bradley, was one of her dad's best friends. Dr Bradley had promised to give Lulu and her friends a special tour.

The kids were gathered in the playground. They were wearing casual clothes instead of their school uniforms.

Lulu was rugged up in her scarf and jacket and a woolly cap. Her best friend Molly had her hands buried deep in her pockets to keep warm. Lauren skipped over, carrying her backpack in one hand.

'Brrrr,' said Lulu. 'It's freezing. I hope the bus comes soon.'

The teachers, Miss Baxter and Miss Donaldson, were organising the children into lines.

'Come on, 3B,' called Miss Baxter. 'It's time to get your names marked off the roll.'

Mum was standing to one side and chatting to the other parents. She had volunteered to help on the excursion. Dad would take Lulu's younger sister Rosie to school later. Her three-year-old brother Gus was spending the day with friends.

‘Fingers crossed I’m in your group, Lulu,’ said Molly. ‘It will be so much fun.’

Lulu nodded, her eyes shining.

‘Dad spoke to Dr Bradley last night,’ said Lulu. ‘She said our group can come and visit her at the zoo’s vet hospital. We might even get to watch an operation.’

Miss Donaldson smiled at them. ‘It sounds like your group is going to have some very special treatment, Lulu. I wish I could come with you.’

At last the big blue bus pulled up at the front gate.

‘Yippety-do,’ cried Lulu.

All the kids piled on the bus and stowed their backpacks under their seats. Lulu, Molly and Lauren sat together. Mum sat beside the other parents. With a rumbling roar, the bus pulled out.

'We're off,' said Lauren. 'I can't wait to get to the zoo.'

'I wonder what animals we'll see today?' asked Molly. 'I hope we see lots of elephants and meerkats.'

'I'd like to see the wombats and the tigers,' said Lulu. 'And the monkeys. They always make me laugh.'

The boy sitting behind Lulu began to make 'oooh-oooh-ahhh-ahhh' noises.

He jumped up and down on his seat, scratching his head with one hand, and under his arm with the other.

Lulu, Lauren and Molly turned around and giggled.

'Max, you make a perfect monkey,' said Lulu.

Max gave a cheeky grin. 'Just call me king of the jungle!'

His friend Daniel chuckled. 'The king of the jungle is the lion. You're more like the jungle joker, Max.'

Max ruffled Daniel's hair, knocking off his cap.

The bus ride took half an hour. The excited kids talked, laughed and joked. The noise was deafening. At last, the bus pulled up at the zoo entrance. The kids piled off.

The teachers divided the year into

eight groups of five. Each group was led by a parent or teacher. Lulu went to stand beside Mum. Miss Baxter called out the names of the other children in their group: Molly, Lauren, Max and Daniel.

'Yay,' cried Molly. 'We're together.' She linked one arm through Lulu's and the other through Lauren's. Max and Daniel gave each other a high five.

Mum smiled at them. 'Looks like I have a fantastic group.'

Mum had her big camera slung around her neck. A clipboard with the zoo map and the plan for the day was tucked under her arm.

Miss Donaldson gave them their instructions. 'Each group will explore the zoo on their own,' she said. 'Please make sure you stay with the adult in charge.

We don't want anyone to get lost.'

Miss Baxter waved a sheaf of papers. 'And here are your treasure hunt sheets. Let's see which group can answer the most questions.'

The sheets had a list of trivia questions about different kinds of animals. Which were the biggest, tallest, sleepiest and most popular animals in the zoo?

Molly took the group's sheet and began to read.

'Which do you think is the most popular animal in the zoo?' asked Molly. 'Maybe the koalas?'

Max shook his head. 'The goofy, gangly giraffes.' He put his arms up high, making himself tall and lanky.

'No, the zany zebras,' added Daniel. He wiggled his eyebrows. 'Or perhaps the loony lions.'

Z Z Z

Lulu thought about it. 'I can't decide,' she said. 'I love them all.'

Miss Donaldson pointed to a green area on the map. 'We'll meet at the park at one o'clock for a picnic.' She checked to make sure everyone was listening. Then with a big grin, she shooed them away. 'Off you go, year three. Have lots of fun!'

The groups set off in various directions. Mum had already studied the map and planned a route.

'We'll go down this path,' said Mum. 'We're meeting Dr Bradley at the vet hospital at ten o'clock. We have time to see some of the animals along the way.'

Lulu threw one of her honey-coloured plaits over her shoulder. 'Come on, everyone,' she called. 'Let's explore.'

Chapter 2

Meerkats

The five children hurtled down the path. Mum followed close behind.

Lulu and Molly looked over the treasure hunt sheet. Molly read out the first question. 'Which is the largest land mammal in the world?'

'Easy,' said Max. 'That would be the *enormous* elephant.'

Lauren looked over Molly's shoulder as she wrote down the answer.

'The next one is much harder. Which animal can eat scorpions because it's immune to venom?' asked Lauren.

Lulu frowned. 'Scorpions are highly venomous,' she said. 'I don't think any animal would want to eat them.'

'We'll have to keep a good eye out,' said Molly.

Ahead and to the left was a low wall. It was painted a dull sand colour. The kids ran to peer over it.

'A mob of meerkats!' cried Lauren.

Inside the enclosure was a large family of about twenty meerkats. They were small grey animals with brownish bands on their fur. They had dark patches around their eyes.

'I love watching the meerkats,' said Molly. 'They almost look like they could talk to us.'

One of the meerkats sat on top of a hillock to keep watch. He made a soft peeping noise. The rest of the family was gathered in the sand. Some were grooming each other. Others were feeding or resting. A couple of youngsters chased each other around the enclosure, tumbling and turning. Mum took photos.

Max and Daniel looked at the sign.

'Meerkats live in the deserts of southern Africa,' Daniel read aloud.

Max pointed to three meerkats who were sitting up on their hind legs. They looked as if they were sunbaking.

'Hey, the dark patches around their eyes act like natural sunglasses,' read Max. 'How cool is that?'

'They look like film stars posing on the red carpet,' joked Lauren.

Everyone laughed.

Lulu read the sign quickly.

'Found it!' she cried. Lulu pointed to the last paragraph. '*Meerkats* can eat scorpions as they are immune to their venom. They also have a high immunity to snake venom.'

'Ugh,' said Molly. She shuddered. 'That's disgusting.'

Lauren took the clipboard and wrote the answer on the treasure hunt sheet.

Max and Daniel ran zigzagging down the path.

'Come on, girls,' said Mum. She folded up the map. 'Let's keep going.'

The boys had stopped outside a big enclosure. It was protected by a tall glass wall. Inside was a mini rainforest with bamboo groves, trees, fallen logs and long, thick grass. To the left was a green pond. The children pressed against the glass.

'What lives in here?' asked Lauren.

'Terrifying tigers,' said Max. He roared and pounced on Daniel for a wrestle.

'The Sumatran tigers,' said Molly, reading the sign. 'The smallest tigers in the world.'

‘There’s a mother with three cubs,’ added Lulu. ‘Two girls and a boy. The male tiger lives next door.’

‘Where are they?’ asked Daniel.

The children looked around the enclosure carefully. There was no sign of any animals. Lulu felt disappointed. She badly wanted to see the tiger cubs.

‘There,’ said Max.

A pair of tawny eyes peered from the shadows. The female tiger stalked out of the undergrowth and into the open. She was dark orange, with thick black stripes and smaller patches of white. The tiger looked around, her long white whiskers twitching.

‘And here are the cubs,’ whispered Lulu.

Three roly-poly cubs tumbled out of the shadows. They pounced and rolled,

ears over tail. They wrestled and played like oversized kittens. They tussled on the side of the pond, then chased each other through the water, splashing and bounding.

'Aren't they beautiful?' asked Lauren.

The mother tiger wandered towards the front of the enclosure, where the five children huddled together. She flopped down in a patch of sun, her back pressed against the glass. Molly jumped away in fright.

Max pressed his palms against the glass. His eyes shone with excitement. 'She's so close I feel like I could pat her.'

The children kept watching the tigers. The male cub was bigger and bolder than the other two. He scrambled up on a fallen log then jumped off, bowling his sister over. Using his claws, he clambered

up a tree trunk, before dropping clumsily to the ground.

The cub hid in the grass and pounced on his mother's tail, as if it were a snake. His mother batted him away with her paw. Then she held him down and licked him with her long, raspy tongue.

The cub wriggled away. His sisters chased him and tripped him over, starting another round of mock-fighting.

Their audience laughed with delight.

'I wish I could get right inside the enclosure,' said Lulu. 'Wouldn't it be lovely to cuddle those cubs?'

'They're adorable,' said Mum. 'But I think the mother tiger would have something to say about you cuddling her babies.'

'Grrrr. She'd eat you all up,' joked Max.

Chapter 3

The Vet Hospital

The group moved on to watch lots of other animals – lions, Asian elephants, giraffes and pandas. They managed to find the answers to several more treasure hunt questions.

'Which is the tallest animal that lives on land?' asked Molly.

'A gigantic giraffe,' said Max. 'The sign said an adult giraffe can be six

metres tall – that's nearly the height of a two-storey building.'

'What do pandas eat?' asked Daniel, as they reached the cuddly black-and-white animals.

'Bamboo makes up ninety-nine per cent of their diet,' answered Lauren.

Mum checked her watch. 'It's nearly ten o'clock. Time to head to the vet hospital.' She pointed towards a narrow path that was nearly hidden by trees. 'This way.'

'I've never noticed this path before,' said Lauren.

In the western corner of the zoo was a big modern building surrounded by trees. This was the vet hospital. Mum pressed the buzzer by the door.

A young nurse in a green uniform answered. A bulging pouch hung at her

waist, held on by a wide shoulder strap.

'Hi,' said Mum. 'I'm Chrissie Bell. This is my daughter Lulu, and her friends from Shelly Beach School. We're here to see Dr Bradley.'

'Come in. I'm Rachael. I work with Dr Bradley.' Rachael opened the door wide and waved them in.

Lulu stared at the bag at Rachael's waist. It was squirming. A tiny orange head emerged and then disappeared again.

Rachael grinned, stroking the bag. 'And this is Linh. She is a baby François' leaf monkey and she loves cuddles.'

The baby stuck its head out of the pouch and stared at the children with big black eyes.

Her name was spelled on the side of her bag.

'Linh is a Vietnamese name,' said Molly. 'It means gentle spirit.'

'That's pretty,' said Lulu.

'François' leaf monkeys come from north-eastern Vietnam and southern China,' said Rachael. She stroked Linh on her furry, orange head. 'They are one of the rarest types of monkeys in the world.'

'Why are they called leaf monkeys?' asked Daniel.

'Because they eat leaves?' suggested Max.

Rachael smiled. 'Exactly right. Linh was born here in the zoo,' she explained. 'But her mother didn't have enough milk for her, so we are rearing her in the nursery. We've been taking turns to sleep

at the vet hospital so we can feed her during the night.'

Lulu felt worried for Linh. 'Doesn't she miss her mother?'

Rachael nodded. 'I carry her around so she doesn't get lonely. François' leaf monkeys are endangered in the wild. We need to make sure Linh has a healthy start in life. We are slowly introducing her back to her family.'

The group followed Rachael down the corridor. The vet hospital was light and clean with lots of large viewing windows. First of all, Rachael led them to a locker room. She showed everyone where to put their backpacks.

Rachael led them into the hospital itself.

The zoo vet hospital was bigger than the Shelly Beach Vet hospital at Lulu's

house. There was no waiting room. The operating theatre was much larger. But the main difference was the animals in the wards. Instead of cats and dogs and rabbits, there were amazing creatures from all over the world.

One room held injured birds, from owls and macaws to kookaburras and flamingos. Another room held glass boxes for the sick reptiles. There were snakes, lizards, turtles and water dragons.

Rachael led the way into another hospital ward. In one corner was a large pen. Inside it, a wombat was asleep on a red beanbag. He was curled up with a teddy bear.

At the sound of the humans coming in, he jumped to his feet. Lulu realised he only had three legs.

'Harry lost his leg in a car accident,'

explained Rachael. 'He can't go back to the wild, but he seems very happy toddling around now. Soon we'll move him out with the other wombats.'

Harry saw Rachael. He ran to the edge of the pen with a lolloping gait. He snuffled and sniffed through the bars.

'He runs awfully fast for a creature with only three legs,' said Max.

'That's because he thinks we're here to give him breakfast,' said Rachael. 'He's very greedy.'

Rachael fetched a container of chopped carrots from the fridge. 'Would you like to feed him?'

Of course, everyone wanted to. Each of the children took a turn to feed Harry through the bars. Harry butted the gate, demanding more food. He made friendly grunts as he crunched and chomped

his way through the carrots. Mum took photos of all the kids with Harry.

'I wish we could take him home,' said Lulu, as Harry tried to nibble her fingers. Lulu looked at her mum with a winning smile. 'He's gorgeous.'

'No way,' said Mum. She threw her hands up in horror. 'Wombats will dig through anything. And just look at the terrible mess he's made eating breakfast.'

There were chunks of carrot all over the floor.

'Never mind,' said Rachael. 'I'll clean it up in a moment. Let's just put Linh away, and then I'll take you to see Dr Bradley.'

Rachael put Linh in a large, warm cage. It was filled with toys. A bunch of tender leaves hung from the roof. Linh began to play with a bright orange ball.

Rachael carefully closed the cage and slid the bolt across.

The group followed Rachael into one of the treatment rooms. Dr Bradley was there, tending to a snake. The vet's long red hair was tied up in a ponytail.

She wore a pale blue shirt over khaki pants.

Dr Bradley smiled and said hello. She gave Lulu and her mum a hug. 'Welcome to our hospital.'

The children crowded around. Dr Bradley was painting antiseptic cream onto some stitches on the snake's belly.

'This is Tammy the carpet python,' said the vet. 'She was brought into the zoo with an unusual problem. Last week we operated to remove three golf balls from her belly. She thought they were chicken eggs and ate them.'

The kids grinned. The snake slithered into a large coil.

'Would you like to hold her, Lulu?' asked Dr Bradley. 'She's not venomous.'

Lulu gave a little skip of excitement. 'Yes, please.'

Dr Bradley showed her where to hold the snake. Lulu was used to helping her dad in the vet hospital. She knew how to hold the reptile calmly and quietly. Lulu was surprised by how heavy the snake was. The other children took turns to stroke the python's slippery scales.

'In another couple of weeks we can release her back into the wild,' said Dr Bradley. 'Hopefully she has learnt not to steal golf balls.'

Rachael took Tammy and went to put her in the reptile ward.

Just then the phone rang. The vet answered.

'Hello? Dr Bradley speaking.' She paused as she listened. A frown crossed her face. 'Okay, I'll be right there.'

Lulu knew that look. It meant that an animal was injured. She wondered what could possibly have happened.

'Is everything all right?' asked Lulu.

'It's Berani, one of the tiger cubs,' said Dr Bradley. 'He's had a fall.'

Chapter 4

Berani

Dr Bradley turned to Mum. 'I'm driving over to the tiger enclosure to check one of the cubs. I can take one passenger. Lulu can come with me if she'd like to.'

'I'm sure she'd love to,' Mum said. She turned to Lulu. 'Wouldn't you, honey bun?'

Lulu nodded. 'Yes, please.'

'How about you walk over with the other children and meet us?' Dr Bradley suggested to Lulu's mum.

Dr Bradley pulled on her jacket and gathered a medical bag full of equipment. She asked Lulu to take a large carry cage. Lulu followed Dr Bradley out through a

side door into the garage. A small buggy was parked there. It had two seats in the front and a bench seat in the back where they put the baggage. Dr Bradley drove very slowly along the path.

The other kids ran as fast as they could back to the Sumatran tiger enclosure.

Dr Bradley parked the buggy around the back. There was a concrete building where the tigers slept. A zookeeper in a khaki uniform was waiting by a locked door. He looked worried.

'Hi, Tom,' called Dr Bradley. 'What happened to Berani?'

'I put his mother away in her sleep pen,' said Tom,

the zookeeper. 'Then when I went in to clean the big enclosure, I found Berani limping. I think he fell when he was climbing one of the trees. He's getting far too curious for his own good.'

'I'll take a look,' said Dr Bradley. 'We'll probably need to take him back to the hospital for an X-ray. When did he last eat?'

'His last solid food was last night,' replied Tom. 'Then he had some milk early this morning.'

'Good, then he should be fine if he needs to have an anaesthetic.'

Dr Bradley lifted the carry cage out of the back of the buggy. She passed it to Tom, then picked up her medical bag. She turned to Lulu.

'I'm sorry, Lulu, but you can't come inside the tiger enclosure,' explained

Dr Bradley. 'Why don't you pop around the front and watch through the glass? Then you can come back with us to the vet hospital afterwards.'

'Sure,' said Lulu. 'Thanks, Dr Bradley.'

Lulu raced around the front of the enclosure.

Through the glass, she could see the biggest cub was standing on three legs. One of the hind legs was lifted in the air, with the foot dangling down. The tiger cub tried to limp. The other two cubs sniffed around curiously.

In a minute, Mum arrived with the other students in the group. They were all huffing from their run. Now Lulu could see Dr Bradley and Tom the zookeeper walking through the long grass towards the tiger cubs. Tom talked softly to the animals.

One of the female cubs trotted towards them. Tom smiled and ruffled her furry head. The tiger rubbed her face against Tom's hand. She licked Tom on the fingers with her long, raspy tongue and made a loud chuffing noise. Tom chuffed back. It reminded Lulu of her family cats, Pickles and Pepper, purring.

Dr Bradley knelt down in the grass beside Berani. Tom crouched beside her and scooped Berani up in his arms. Carefully and gently, Dr Bradley examined the tiger's hind leg. Then Dr Bradley wrapped the cub in a towel and put him inside the carry cage.

Tom picked up the cage. Dr Bradley waved to Lulu to meet them around the back. They set off towards the rear of the enclosure, followed by the two smaller cubs. Lulu ran around to meet them.

Tom got into the buggy's passenger seat and cradled the cage on his lap. Lulu could see two tufted ears flicking back

and forth. Lulu squeezed in the back where the cage had been.

Dr Bradley drove back to the vet hospital slowly and parked the buggy.

A low rumble came from the carry cage on Tom's lap.

'It's all right, Berani,' soothed Tom. 'Our clever vet will have you chasing around in no time.'

'You bet,' Dr Bradley said, smiling at Lulu. 'Have you ever seen an operation on a tiger cub?'

Lulu shot out of the back of the buggy. 'Really? Can we really, truly watch?'

Chapter 5

The Operation

At the vet hospital, Tom and Dr Bradley took Berani into the operating theatre. Lulu joined the other children and watched through the viewing window. Mum explained to them what was going on.

'First they'll give him an anaesthetic,' said Mum. 'Then they'll take an X-ray of his hind leg.'

Tom held Berani tightly while the

cub was given an injection. In a few moments, Berani was fast asleep on the stainless steel operating table. He had a tube in his mouth to help him breathe. Once Berani was safely asleep, Dr Bradley and Tom came out to join the watching children.

Inside the operating theatre, Rachael set up the X-ray machine. She worked the machine from a special booth.

Dr Bradley turned on a computer on the bench. The children gathered around to watch.

'Berani is nearly three months old,' said Dr Bradley as she worked on the computer. 'His name means brave and he is always getting into trouble. It doesn't surprise me that he took a tumble.'

'We saw him climbing a tree trunk this morning,' said Lauren. 'He jumped

down then, but it didn't look like he had hurt himself.'

'We need to take very special care of Berani,' said Tom. 'He and his sisters were the first Sumatran tiger cubs born in our zoo. He is one of only about four hundred Sumatran tigers left in the world. They are critically endangered. This means we need to work very hard to save them from extinction.'

Lulu felt a cold shiver run up her spine. 'Extinction? You mean the Sumatran tigers might die out altogether?'

She watched the tiger cub lying on the operating table. He looked small and helpless.

'Not if we can help it,' said Dr Bradley. Her voice sounded serious. 'Zoos around the world are working

together on a breeding program to save the Sumatran tiger.'

'When Berani and his sisters are grown up, we will send them to live in different zoos in other countries,' said Tom. 'Then they can have cubs of their own.'

Some black-and-white pictures came up on the computer screen. They were X-ray images of Berani's leg bones. Dr Bradley enlarged one.

'Look there, Lulu,' she said. 'What can you see?'

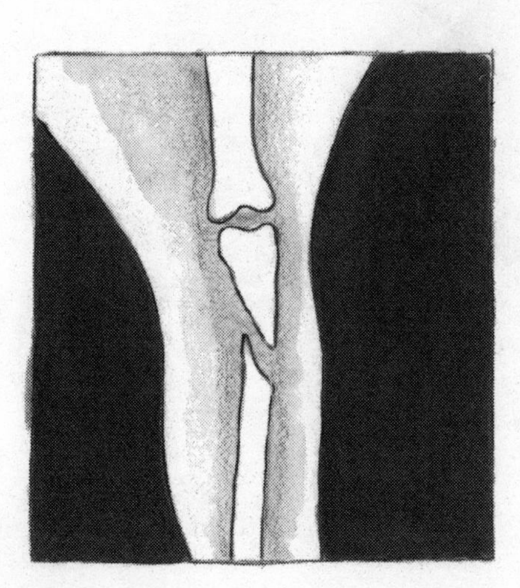

'It looks like he has a broken bone,' said Lulu. She pointed to an image of his fractured thighbone.

'That's right. We call that bone the femur,' explained Dr Bradley. 'To fix that we'll need to do an operation with a metal plate and some screws.'

The vet pointed to the X-ray. 'I'll make a small cut here and then straighten the bone. We'll use the

metal plate to hold the bone in place while it heals.'

Lulu nodded.

'Now let's get to work,' said Dr Bradley. She went to get changed. Tom stayed behind and watched anxiously.

Dr Bradley and Rachael put on sterile surgical gowns over their clothes. They scrubbed their hands and wore hats, masks and gloves.

The children could see everything through the window. First, Rachael made sure Berani was getting plenty of oxygen through a tube. He was linked to a monitor that checked his heart rate. Dr Bradley shaved his leg and swabbed the skin with antiseptic. Rachael passed her the instruments she needed. Dr Bradley straightened the bone. She used screws to hold the metal plate in place.

Finally the wound was stitched up.

When the operation was complete, Berani was placed in a warm, well-padded box. He was still asleep.

Dr Bradley pulled off her gloves, mask and hat. She smiled at the children through the window. 'Would you like to come in and take a closer look?'

'Yes, please,' cried Lulu.

Everyone filed into the theatre and gathered around the operating table.

'Berani will wake up soon. Would you like to pat him?' asked Dr Bradley. 'You can stroke him along the top of his head. Just be very gentle.'

Lulu ran her fingers over his orange-and-black striped body. His fur felt a bit coarser than the cats at home.

Dr Bradley showed the children one of his paws. 'Tigers have webbing between their toes to help them swim. They are great swimmers, which is unusual for big cats.'

Berani had soft pads on the base of his paws and needle-sharp claws.

'And look at this. Can you see his false eyes?'

Lulu wasn't sure what the vet meant. 'What are false eyes?'

Dr Bradley pointed. On the back of each rounded ear was a large circular white spot.

'The spots look like eyes, which helps scare off predators from behind,' explained the vet.

'Tigers really do have eyes in the back of their heads,' joked Lulu. 'Just like Mum.'

Dr Bradley chuckled. Berani's tufted ears twitched.

'He's waking up,' said Dr Bradley. 'It's time for Berani to go into the intensive care unit.'

Lulu looked down at Berani, who was sleeping peacefully.

What an amazing experience to watch an operation on a tiger cub, thought Lulu. *How could our zoo adventure get any better than that?*

Chapter 6

Missing Monkey

Tom helped Rachael carry Berani to the intensive care ward. When Berani was safely tucked away, Tom left to go back to work. A few minutes later, Rachael poked her head around the door. She looked worried.

'Has someone moved Linh, the leaf monkey?' Rachael asked. 'She's not in her cage.'

'No,' said Dr Bradley with a frown.

'When did you last see her?'

Rachael thought for a moment. 'I put her away just before you went to get Berani. When I went to check on her, the cage door was open and she was gone.'

'She must be here somewhere,' said Dr Bradley. 'Why don't we all have a really good look for her?'

First they checked Linh's cage again. The door was wide open. Inside were her water bowl and her orange ball. Other toys had been thrown out onto the floor.

'I know I closed the door,' said Rachael. She looked as though she might cry. 'I'm always so careful with the cage doors.'

'I know you are,' said Dr Bradley. 'Perhaps Linh is more cunning than we thought. Monkeys are very clever at opening locks and doors. She's only a baby so we thought she'd be safe.'

The kids split into teams: Molly and Lauren, Mum and Lulu, Daniel and Max. They searched high on top of the cages and low under benches. They looked in Harry's enclosure and in the aviary. With pounding hearts they searched the reptile room. Linh was nowhere to be found.

Rachael was very upset. 'What if we can't find her? I'll never forgive myself.'

Berani the cub was waking up now. He cried a mini roar when he discovered

that he had a big bandage on his leg.

'It's all right, Berani,' soothed Lulu as she passed. 'Right now, we have more important things to worry about.'

Max gave a shout from the locker room. Lulu and Molly rushed in. There was chaos.

Someone – or something – had opened all the backpacks. Hats and scarves were strewn all over the floor.

Paper had been torn into little pieces and sprinkled like snow. Lunch boxes and drink bottles had been overturned. Lulu's lunch box was open. There were nibble marks on the grapes. The salad sandwich had been opened and the lunch paper was crumpled into a ball.

'Oh my goodness,' said Lulu. 'I think I know who has been causing trouble here.'

'Linh, the gentle spirit leaf monkey,' said Molly. 'Perhaps that wasn't such a good name for her after all.'

Everyone searched the locker room, but Linh was nowhere to be found. Molly and Max set to work to tidy the mess. Mum swept the floor, while Rachael fetched the mop.

Lulu was thirsty. She decided to get some water from the staff room and

search in there. The staff room had a long wooden table surrounded by chairs. There was a small kitchen with a sink, fridge, kettle and a microwave. A large window looked out over the zoo gardens.

On the bench was a plate of smashed chocolate biscuit crumbs. Lulu found a glass and filled it with water from the tap.

A funny noise sounded. It was a soft chittering up near the ceiling.

Lulu wrinkled her forehead. What creature would make that noise? She listened carefully as she stood by the sink.

The sound seemed to be coming from above the kitchen cupboards. Lulu began to investigate. She climbed onto a chair and then the bench. She stood upright on the bench and peered at the top of the cupboards.

A dark shape was huddled at the far end. It had orange fur on its head and legs. The fur on its back was darker.

'Linh,' whispered Lulu. 'Is that you?'

The baby monkey turned towards Lulu, staring at her with big black eyes. She looked frightened.

Lulu walked slowly along the kitchen bench, talking softly.

'It's all right, Linh,' she whispered. 'Time to come down now.'

Lulu was halfway along when the leaf monkey charged straight towards her.

She leaped for Lulu and landed on top of her head. The monkey gripped tightly. A long tail curled in Lulu's face. Lulu thought she must look funny, as though she was wearing a furry monkey hat.

'Hello, Linh,' murmured Lulu. 'There's a good girl.'

Lulu gently lifted the monkey off her head and cuddled her close to her chest. The monkey buried her head against Lulu, making soft squeaking noises.

'Good girl,' crooned Lulu. 'It's good to see you safe and sound. Let's take you back. Everyone is so worried about you.'

Dad always said that baby animals felt safer if they were wrapped up in something soft. Lulu found a pile of folded towels on a shelf. She carefully wrapped a towel around Linh and carried her out the door.

In the corridor, Lulu saw Rachael. The woman was hurrying along looking pale and stressed.

'Rachael?' Lulu called softly. 'Look who I found.'

'Linh!' cried Rachael. She flushed pink with happiness and relief. 'Oh, thank you, Lulu. Wherever did you find her?'

Lulu carried Linh back into the ward while she explained how she had found the baby monkey. She stroked Linh's head. The monkey gazed about with big wide eyes. Linh lifted her tiny front paws and patted Lulu on the chin.

'Oh, she is simply adorable,' said Lulu. 'I wish we could take her home.'

Rachael opened the cage door. 'She certainly is,' she agreed. 'But if you took her home, Linh wouldn't learn how to be a proper monkey, would she? I hope next time you come to the zoo, Linh will be living with her mother and the rest of her group.'

Lulu thought about it. 'Yes, I'd rather she was with her family.'

Lulu gave Linh one last cuddle, then put her back in her cage.

This time Rachael made sure that the cage was double-locked.

Mum came in with Molly. Everyone gathered around the cage to look at the rescued runaway.

'I'm so glad the leaf monkey is safe, honey bun,' said Mum. 'But we really have to go now. We are running late to meet all the other kids for a picnic in the park. They will be wondering what on earth has happened to us.'

Chapter 7

Picnic Feast

Lulu hung back. She didn't want to leave the hospital and all the fascinating patients there. Everyone went to say goodbye to Dr Bradley and Rachael.

'Perhaps I could skip lunch and stay here?' Lulu asked her mum. 'I'm not at all hungry.'

Mum laughed. 'I don't think so, Lulu. We have to go or we'll miss the seal show after lunch.'

Lulu looked disappointed. Dr Bradley smiled at her.

'Don't worry, Lulu,' said the vet. 'Perhaps you can come back to visit soon. Then you can see how Berani and Linh are getting on. And I'd love to see the rest of the Bell family too.'

Lulu turned to her mum. 'Oh, could we, please? Can we come back *really* soon?'

'I'm sure we can, honey bun,' said Mum. 'We'll bring Dad and Rosie and Gus along too.'

Dr Bradley walked them to the door. Just as they were leaving, Lulu had a thought.

'We haven't finished the treasure hunt trivia,' Lulu reminded everyone. 'But perhaps Dr Bradley can help us with the last two questions?'

Dr Bradley nodded. 'I'll try. What do you want to know?'

'All right,' said Lulu. 'Which is the sleepiest animal in the zoo?'

'Ah, that would be the koalas,' said Dr Bradley. 'They sleep for up to twenty-two hours each day.'

Lauren wrote down the answer.

'And lastly, which is the most popular animal in the zoo?'

Dr Bradley laughed. 'That's easy. We did some research and asked thousands of people which was their favourite animal. And do you know what most people said?'

Lulu shook her head. 'At first, we thought it might be the elephants or the giraffes or the koalas,' she said. 'But now, I can't choose between Linh the leaf monkey and Berani the tiger cub.'

Dr Bradley winked at Lulu. She leaned over and whispered the answer in her ear. Lulu grinned with delight.

Then everyone hurried outside and down towards the park. The other year three students and the teachers and parents were just finishing their lunch. Miss Baxter was relieved to see Lulu's group finally arrive.

The park was sheltered and warm. The wide grassy lawn was surrounded by a low sandstone wall. Purple lavender blossomed in the flower beds, filling the air with its sweet scent. A turquoise peacock strutted past. He lifted his tail in a gorgeous display, like a green-and-blue patterned fan.

'Look at those colours,' said Mum, snapping a photograph. 'He's exquisite.'

Max and Daniel went over to a group of boys sitting on the wall. Max immediately began to entertain them all with his monkey impersonation. He leaped and cavorted. He scratched his head and made 'oooh-oooh-aaah-aaah' noises. The boys chuckled and giggled as Daniel told them about their adventures at the vet hospital.

Lulu, Molly and Lauren went to sit with Mum in the sun beside the lavender hedge. Everyone opened their lunch boxes except Lulu.

Linh the monkey had destroyed most of Lulu's lunch, so she shared a lamb-and-tomato sandwich with Mum. Molly gave her some of her spicy noodle salad with lime juice and mint. They finished off the meal by passing around juicy red strawberries. The fruit was sweet and delicious.

'This is wonderful,' said Lulu. She leaned back against the grass. 'Do you think this has been the best excursion ever?'

'Absolutely,' said Lauren and Molly together.

Chapter 8

Return to the Zoo

One Friday a few weeks later, Dad organised to finish work early. Mum, Dad and Gus came to pick Lulu and Rosie up from school.

Gus was wearing his all-in-one tiger suit, in honour of the trip. Lulu and Rosie wore their warm jackets and scarves over their school uniforms.

As they got in the car, Lulu wriggled with excitement.

'Hurray,' said Lulu. 'I'm so glad we're going back to the zoo. I can't wait to show you Berani and Linh.'

Dr Bradley met them at the zoo entrance. She gave everyone a big hug.

'Come this way,' invited Dr Bradley. 'I want to show you our new François' leaf monkey enclosure.'

Dr Bradley led the way towards the Asian rainforest trail. Lulu, Rosie and Gus ran from enclosure to enclosure so they could see the different animals on the way. They passed the orang-utans, Asian elephants, gibbons and tapirs.

They stopped at an enclosure surrounded by a glass wall. It was filled with tall trees, vines and fallen logs. Thick leaf litter carpeted the ground. Ten leaf monkeys were inside. Unlike Linh, these monkeys were black with tufts of white whiskers on their faces.

Some were foraging for leaves and fruit. Some were resting and grooming each other high in the branches.

'Can you see Linh?' asked Dr Bradley.

Lulu noticed that one black-and-white François' leaf monkey was sitting on a high branch. Tucked in her arms was

a smaller monkey with a bright orange head.

'There she is,' cried Lulu. 'That's Linh, the baby monkey who escaped.'

'She has been living with her family for the last few days,' said Dr Bradley. 'But we still give her bottles of milk several times a day.'

Linh scrambled out of her mother's arms. She galloped along the branch, her tail curled above her head.

'But Linh doesn't look like the other monkeys,' said Rosie. 'She has an orange head.'

'She will stay orange for a few months, then she will turn black like her mother,' explained Dr Bradley. 'She is quite an acrobat these days.'

The monkey grabbed a hanging rope and swung out high above the ground.

She leaped through the air and landed safely on another branch. She swung and jumped from pole to tree all the way back to her mother.

'It's so wonderful that we can come and watch these rare animals,' said Dad. He turned to Dr Bradley. 'You are doing a fantastic job here at the zoo. It's so important that endangered animals like these can survive.'

Dr Bradley smiled. 'For a while there, we thought we'd lost one baby leaf monkey. Luckily, Lulu found her before she wandered too far.'

Mum hugged Lulu. 'Our Lulu has an amazing knack for finding lost and injured animals.'

Lulu felt a thrill of pride.

Gus was impatient to be off. 'Go see tigey.'

Dr Bradley laughed. 'You make a great tiger yourself, Gus.'

The vet led the way to another rainforest enclosure. Inside, the mother tiger was lying in a patch of wintry sunshine. Three roly-poly tiger cubs tumbled all over her.

'The biggest one's Berani,' cried Lulu. 'Look, he's hardly limping at all.'

'I checked his leg this morning and it's healing beautifully,' said Dr Bradley.

'The cubs are gorgeous,' said Rosie. 'I love the littlest one with the white patch on her tummy.'

Gus galloped around pretending to be a tiger cub. He butted into Mum's leg and growled ferociously. Dad scooped

him up and swung him high in the air. Gus sat up on Dad's shoulders and looked down at the real cubs.

Berani noticed the humans and lolloped towards them. He rubbed his furry face against the window. He jumped up, resting his front paws against the glass. Lulu pressed her hands

against the window and pretended to rub his tummy. She imagined she could feel the warmth of his body through the cool glass.

Lulu turned towards Mum and Dad. 'Can you guess which animals in the zoo are the most popular?' she asked.

'The pandas?' guessed Dad.

'The monkeys?' guessed Mum.

Lulu shook her head. She gave Dr Bradley a big smile.

'The tiger cubs,' announced Lulu.

Lulu's Zoo Treasure Hunt Trivia

1. Which is the largest mammal that lives on land?
2. Which is the tallest animal that lives on land?
3. How many Sumatran tigers are left in the wild?
4. How big is a kangaroo when it's born?

5. What is the sleepiest animal?

6. What do pandas eat?

7. Which animal has a pouch that faces backwards?

8. Name one of the few animals that can use tools?

9. Why are flamingos pink?

10. How many insects can an anteater eat in a single day?

11. Which is the fastest animal on land?

Answers

1. The African elephant can weigh up to 12,000 kilograms.
2. The giraffe can grow to six metres tall. That's the height of a two-storey building.
3. There are only about 400 Sumatran tigers left in the wild. They are extremely endangered.
4. A newborn kangaroo is about the size of a human thumbnail.
5. Koalas sleep about 18 to 22 hours per day.
6. Ninety-nine per cent of the panda's diet is bamboo.
7. The wombat's pouch faces backwards. This is so their joeys are protected from flying dirt when the mother digs burrows.
8. The chimpanzee uses tools.
9. The flamingo's pink colouring comes from the food they eat.
10. An anteater can eat up to 30,000 insects in a single day.
11. The cheetah is the fastest animal on land. It can reach speeds of more than 100 kilometres per hour.

Lulu Bell and the Pyjama Party

Molly, Sam and Ebony the kitten are staying the night for a pyjama party. Yay! Lulu is looking forward to stories and games and snacks.

But it's a busy night for Dad's vet hospital. An orphaned wallaby joey needs care and when a mother dog arrives at the vet hospital ready to have her puppies, Dad needs Lulu and Molly's help – even if they're still in their pyjamas!

Out now

Read all the Lulu Bell books

Lulu Bell and the Birthday Unicorn

Lulu Bell and the Fairy Penguin

Lulu Bell and the Cubby Fort

Lulu Bell and the Moon Dragon

Lulu Bell and the Circus Pup

Lulu Bell and the Sea Turtle

Lulu Bell and the Tiger Cub

Lulu Bell and the Pyjama Party

Lulu Bell and the Christmas Elf

November 2014

About the Author

Belinda Murrell grew up in a vet hospital and Lulu Bell is based on some of the adventures she shared with her own animals. When she was a teenager, Belinda spent a week working with the vet at Western Plains Zoo, a close family friend. After studying Literature at Macquarie University, Belinda worked as a travel journalist, editor and technical writer. A few years ago, she began to write stories for her own three children – Nick, Emily and Lachlan. Belinda's books include the Sun Sword fantasy trilogy, timeslip tales *The Locket of Dreams*, *The Ruby Talisman* and *The Ivory Rose*, and Australian historical tales *The Forgotten Pearl*, *The River Charm* and *The Sequin Star*. Belinda is also an ambassador for Room to Read and Books in Homes.

www.belindamurrell.com.au

About the Illustrator

Serena Geddes spent six years working with a fabulously mad group of talented artists at Walt Disney Studios in Sydney before embarking on the path of picture book illustration in 2009. She works both traditionally and digitally and has illustrated eighteen books, ranging from picture books to board books to junior novels.

www.serenageddes.com.au